THE ADVENTURES OF MR. MUFFINS

Written by Bill Pagum
Illustrated by Leona Hosack

To Mr. Muffins
and all the pets
that care for us.

Mr. Muffins sat on the top of the soft padded couch and looked out the window. He was the new dog in the neighborhood, a small Yorkie, looking for adventure. Iris and Hunter walked over to greet him. They saw the moving truck and wanted to meet a new friend. Iris had one eye and Hunter was a hound dog.

Mr. Muffins was at the window and saw them. He barked and barked and scratched the window glass with his paws. Iris and Hunter stopped. They went home confused because they just wanted to play.

Then Mr. Muffins ran through the house and went wild. He shredded a sock, tore into the tissue basket, and pulled the cloth off the kitchen table. The salt shaker hit him on the head and Mr. Muffins cried.

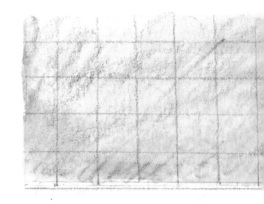

The next day, Mr. Muffins went on a car ride in his crate to dog school. At school he learned to stay still, be quiet, sit, and give paw. The teacher pulled him off his feet with a long leash when he misbehaved. Mr. Muffins was a fast learner.

At home, Mr. Muffins met Mr. Elephant and Mr. Moose, his new toys. He chased Mr. Elephant around the room and played retrieve when Mr. Moose was thrown down the hall. Mr. Elephant was his crate buddy.

Outside, Mr. Muffins barked at the squirrel. He did not like the squirrel eating bird food. His friends the Cardinal and Woodpecker perched at the feeder quite often. He tugged on his rope again and again very hard. The rope frayed a bit. An Owl and Coyote watched him with interest.

One day later in the week, Mr. Muffins saw the Squirrel again and really tugged hard on the rope and it broke. Mr. Muffins was free. He chased the Squirrel until it disappeared up a tree. He found himself deep in the woods just as the sun set in the west. Mr. Muffins was lost.

For a while, Mr. Muffins enjoyed being lost. He had no school or crate or anyone telling him what to do. He smelled brand new scents in the woods. Mr. Muffins walked further along, then slower, and slower. Now it was dark and cold. Mr. Muffins was tired and hungry.

Next Mr. Muffins stopped and listened. His ears perked up and his nose caught the night breeze. Something was up. He was not alone in the woods. Many creatures were coming out to meet him. Mr. Muffins was scared.

He saw the eyes first. The Owl hooted and the Coyote howled. They were hungry. Mr. Muffins saw them and backed up against a big bush. The Coyote growled with big teeth and the Owl jumped down to the lowest branch of the tree above.

Mr. Muffins backed up. He felt the bush behind him and he kept pushing against it as he retreated from the Coyote. Then the Coyote tensed and jumped and Mr. Muffins tried to duck and hug the ground. The big branch behind him released with great force and hit the Coyote right in the face. She howled wildly and fled and the Owl took flight.

Frightened, Mr. Muffins jumped and landed in a leaf covered hole. He fell deep inside. He went to sleep with the moist leaves covering him up. He forgot about being lost deep in the woods among wild things.

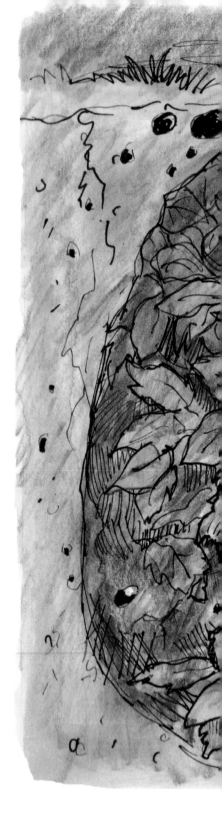

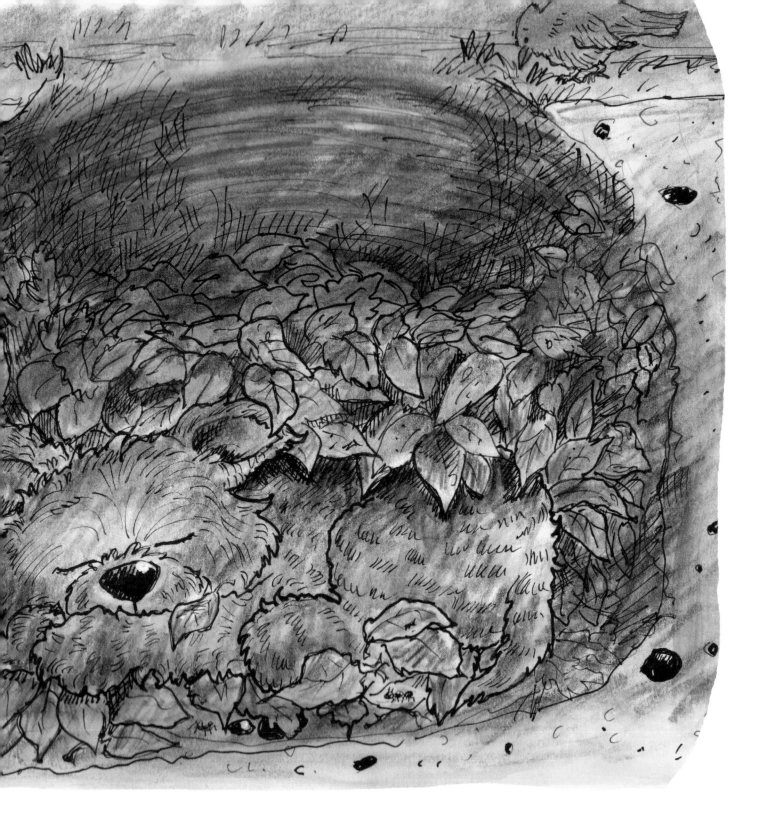

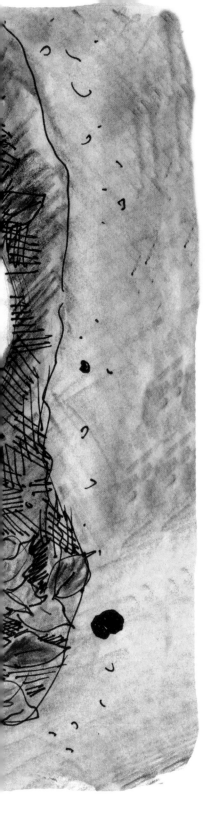

In the morning, he woke
up hungry and thirsty.
Mr. Muffins missed his
friends Mr. Elephant and
Mr. Moose. Mr. Muffins
cried. Then he whimpered,
next he started barking and
howling. He was very sad.

Suddenly Mr. Muffins heard a noise. A scratching sound. He barked again. He heard a yelp. Then he saw daylight. Hunter! He saw his neighbor the hound dog. Hunter dug some more and Mr. Muffins climbed out—he was free again. Iris was there too. Iris brought some food and shared with Mr. Muffins. He gave Iris a little kiss.

Hunter yelped again. Time
to go. Mr. Muffins barked
too. He agreed. Hunter led the
way, Iris followed, and Mr.
Muffins jumped in behind
Iris. Mr. Muffins finally
knew his place in the pack.
They headed toward the voices
at the edge of the woods.

The Adventures of Mr. Muffins
Copyright © 2017 by Bill Pagum
Illustrated by Leona Hosack

Published by Piscataqua Press
an imprint of RiverRun Bookstore

ISBN: 978-1-944393-68-7

CPSIA information can be obtained at www.ICGtesting.com
Printed in the USA
BVIW12n1639141117
500333BV00001B/1

* 9 7 8 1 9 4 4 3 9 3 6 8 7 *